The Green Men of Gressingham

by Philip Ardagh

ILLUSTRATED BY MIKE PHILLIPS

Librarian Reviewer
Kathleen Baxter
Children's Literature Consultant, formerly with Anoka County Library, MN
BA from College of Saint Catherine, St. Paul, MN
MA in Library Science, University of Minnesota, MN

Reading Consultant
Elizabeth Stedem
Educator/Consultant, Colorado Springs, CO
MA in Elementary Education, University of Denver, CO

STONE ARCH BOOKS
Minneapolis   San Diego

First published in the United States in 2006
by Stone Arch Books,
151 Good Counsel Drive, P.O. Box 669,
Mankato, Minnesota 56002.
www.stonearchbooks.com

Published by arrangement with
Barrington Stoke Ltd, Edinburgh.

Library of Congress Cataloging-in-Publication Data
Ardagh, Philip.
        The Green Men of Gressingham / by Philip Ardagh; illustrated by Mike
Phillips.
        p. cm. — (Pathway Books)
        Summary: Tom Dashwood looks forward to becoming a knight, but on
his way to start his training, he is kidnapped by Robyn-in-the-Hat and the
Green Men of Gressingham, a band of outlaws protesting unfair taxes.
        ISBN-13: 978-1-59889-000-6 (hardcover)
        ISBN-10: 1-59889-000-X (hardcover)
        [1. Robbers and outlaws—Fiction. 2. Kidnapping—Fiction. 3. Middle
Ages—Fiction. 4. Knights and knighthood—Fiction. 5. Great Britain—
History—Richard I, 1189–1199—Fiction. 6. Humorous stories.] I. Phillips,
Mike, 1961– ill. II. Title. III. Series.
PZ7.A6776Gre 2006
[Fic]—dc22   2005026579

Cover Illustration by Brett Hawkins

1 2 3 4 5 6 11 10 09 08 07 06

Printed in the United States of America.

Table of Contents

Robyn-in-the-Hat

Fidget

Friendly

Big Jim

Tom

Introduction

Meet the Green Men of Gressingham, a band of robbers and outlaws who dress in brown. Why brown? It's cheaper than green and hides the dirt better.

The leader of this band is Robyn-in-the-Hat. Then there's Big Jim, Friendly, Fidget, and many more. They're going to take someone prisoner — Tom Dashwood, the hero of this tale!

Chapter 1

Up before the Rooster Crows

Tom Dashwood was up before the rooster crowed that Friday morning. The servants had only been up an hour when he came into the great hall.

They cleared away the straw they used for their beds, and Cook put some breakfast on the long table.

It wasn't normal for Tom and his family to have breakfast together. But this was not a normal Friday.

The day before, a big man had come to the Manor House. He wore a floppy hat that looked like a soft, round loaf of bread. His name was Able Morris. He had been sent by Tom's uncle, Lord Dashwood, to take Tom back to Dashwood Castle, so he could train to be a page.

In those days, a boy had to train to be a page and then a squire, and then at last he could become a real knight.

Tom had been so excited he could not sleep. He always longed to go to Dashwood Castle to train to be a knight. Now that day had come.

He had spent the night thinking about mock battles. He could hear the sound of horses' hooves and the cheers of the crowds.

Tom's mom, Lady Ann, planned a
family breakfast to say goodbye. This
way she could spend a little more time
with her son before he left. She was
happy for him but sad to see him go.
Most moms are like that.

Everyone drank juice for breakfast.
They never drank water from their well
because it was a horrid, brown color
and tasted like mud.

Now the day had come at last. Tom's mom wasn't hungry, and her eyes were red. She'd been awake all night, thinking of her little boy who would soon leave home.

"Let's drink to my son," said Tom's dad, Sir Simon. "To Tom, as he sets out to win honor and glory!"

"Honor and glory," Able Morris said after him, and everyone lifted their goblets to their lips. Tom felt so proud that his face glowed bright red.

"We must say goodbye now, Sir Simon," said Able Morris. "Tom and I have a long way to go."

Everyone, even the servants, went to see Tom off.

Lady Ann's handkerchief was wet with tears. "Be brave and true, Tom," she said.

Tom's dad gave him a hug. Able Morris got onto his huge horse, Ferdy, and pulled Tom up to sit behind him.

Tom hoped that they wouldn't ride too fast. He could not put his arms around Able Morris's waist. It was much too big.

Able Morris turned around and looked at Tom. "It's time we were off!" he said.

Everyone yelled "goodbye" and "good luck" at them as they set off to Dashwood Castle.

Chapter 2

Gressingham Forest

At first they passed places Tom knew well. He'd been to them with his dad — the village, the church, the field where the Harvest Festival was held each year.

Then they rode past places that Tom had only seen from far off.

When Tom looked back, he could no longer see his home. All he could see was the very top of the church steeple.

"We'll be coming to Gressingham
Forest soon, Master Tom," said Able.
"There's a band of outlaws in there.
Don't say a word, and hold on tight.
We may have to ride off fast."

Tom was both scared and excited.
He had only left home this morning,
and here he was in the middle of
an adventure!

Then the road went into the thick
forest. Tom's mouth went dry as Able
Morris gave Ferdy a kick.

They went on and on, deep into
the forest.

Tom looked from left to right. The
trees and bushes were dark and thick.

Outlaws and robbers won't bother
with us, he thought to himself.

Outlaws only want to attack rich people with jewels or bags of gold.

He was wrong!

There was a sound like the hoot of an owl, but owls don't hoot in the daytime. It must be a signal!

It was. A band of men dressed in brown surrounded them.

The tallest man Tom had ever seen came up to them. "We have visitors!" boomed the man in a deep voice. "Let's welcome them, men."

All at once Tom was dragged off the horse and stuffed into a sack.

The outlaws must have had some huge sacks because they found one that fit Able Morris.

Able was a lot larger than Tom, and he fought a lot. It took six outlaws to get him into his sack. They stuffed his hat into his mouth to stop him from shouting some very rude words.

Tom could hear all this going on, but he couldn't see anything. The sack he was in had been tied at the top with a rope.

It was not a bad sack. It wasn't too thick, so there was some light inside. And it wasn't that itchy stuff that makes you want to scratch all the time.

Tom would have liked a pillow in his sack. But he didn't have too much to moan about — except that he had been kidnapped.

If he couldn't think of a plan to escape, he might never get to be a knight after all!

Tom stopped shouting, "Let me out!" and thought he might get a little sleep. But then the sack was lifted up, and the rope around the top was untied. The next moment Tom was tipped onto the mossy ground.

Tom blinked and looked around. He was deep in the forest, and the outlaws were all around him. They were armed with big sticks, and bows and arrows.

"Who are you?" Tom asked. "And what have you done with Able?"

The very tall man laughed. "We do the asking," he boomed. The other men laughed, too.

"My name is Tom Dashwood," said Tom. "My parents are Sir Simon and Lady Ann Dashwood."

"So Lord Dashwood of Dashwood Castle is your uncle?" said a rather jolly outlaw.

Like the others, he was dressed in brown.

"Yes, he is," said Tom with pride. "So I think you'd better let me and Able Morris go. My uncle will send out a whole army of knights to look for me."

"Oooh! I'm shaking all over," said the tall man as he grinned.

"I bet you're not brave enough to tell me your names!" snapped Tom.

"No one tells me I'm not brave," said the man. "My name is Big Jim!"

"And we are the Green Men of Gressingham," he added.

Tom looked around at the band of men. They were all sizes, and they all wore the same brown clothes.

"The Green Men of Gressingham?" asked Tom. Big Jim nodded. "Then why are you all dressed in brown?"

"It hides the dirt better," said the jolly one. "We don't get much time to wash our clothes. My name is Friendly."

Friendly held out his hand for Tom to shake.

Tom liked Friendly even though he was an outlaw. He shook his hand.

"I do think it would be best for all of us if you let me and Able go," Tom said.

"Not so fast!" said Big Jim. "What are you doing in Gressingham Forest?"

"I'm on my way to Dashwood Castle," said Tom. "I'm going to learn to be a knight."

He looks friendly to me.

"That castle is a bad place," said Friendly.

"For outlaws, perhaps," said Tom, "but not for good, honest people!"

"When were you there last?" asked another outlaw, the one called Fidget.

"I've never been there," Tom had to admit.

Chapter 3

Robyn-in-the-Hat

"We can't blame the boy for his uncle's crimes if he's never even been to Dashwood Castle," said Friendly. "I say we should let him go!"

Now Tom really liked him.

"And I say we should keep him here and ask for ransom," said Big Jim. "Lord Dashwood will pay well to get Tom back alive."

Boo! Hiss! thought Tom.

"We could do with a few bags of gold!" cried another.

"That's it, then," said Big Jim. "We'll keep Tom, and we'll set Able Morris free. He can go and tell Lord Dashwood that Tom is our prisoner."

"We must ask the boss about that," said Friendly. The others said nothing.

Tom could hear Able inside his sack, under a far-off tree. "I thought you were the boss," said Tom to Big Jim.

"Er," began Big Jim. "I'm in charge until Robyn-in-the-Hat gets back."

"And Robyn is your leader?"

"Don't you know anything?" asked Friendly. "People sing songs about the great deeds of Robyn-in-the-Hat and the Green Men of Gressingham!"

"I don't get out much," Tom admitted. "I've never been this far from home before. Any new song takes ages to get to us."

"Well, you're a brave one," said a voice behind him.

Tom looked around to see a woman in an odd brown hat come out from behind a bush.

"I don't think much of any of you!" she exclaimed. "Not one of you outlaws saw me creeping up on you! I've heard every word you've said for the past ten minutes. What if I'd been a spy for Lord Dashwood?"

"But you're not. You're Robyn," grinned Friendly.

"So no harm's been done!" said Big Jim.

"So your uncle is Lord Dashwood," Robyn said to Tom.

He looked at Robyn-in-the-Hat. Her hat was very odd indeed. It was half hat and half mask. A flap with two holes came down over the top part of her face. Through the holes Tom could see two shining blue eyes.

"Why do you wear a mask when none of your men do?" asked Tom.

"They are full-time outlaws, Tom, but I lead two lives," Robyn told him. "It helps me in my work."

"Why should I believe a word you say," asked Tom, "when you told all those lies about my uncle — ?"

Big Jim growled. "We are outlaws, but we don't tell lies about Lord Dashwood," he said.

"Dashwood Castle and its lands were once a happy place," said Friendly. "But not any more."

"There are all these unfair new taxes. Your uncle has sent out his marshal, Guppy, to collect them," said Robyn-in-the-Hat. "The poor people who work on your uncle's lands cannot pay the taxes."

Tom didn't know what to think. Why would Robyn and the Green Men of Gressingham lie to him?

"The castle's dungeon is full of good, honest people who tried to stand up to your uncle," Robyn told Tom.

"Able Morris didn't tell me any of this," said Tom.

"Well, he's your uncle's man, isn't he?" said Robyn.

Then there was another hoot, just like the first one. Big Jim put his huge hand over Tom's mouth.

Fidget pressed the tip of his sword against Able Morris's sack. "Stay silent, or you'll be sorry," he hissed.

So Able Morris was silent for the first time since he'd been taken prisoner. Now every Green Man of Gressingham was armed and ready.

Robyn-in-the-Hat and her band of outlaws were amazed to see a man on a donkey.

He had been hurt.

"It's Max the Miller!" cried Friendly, and he rushed forward to help the man down from the donkey.

"What's the matter, Max?" Robyn wanted to know.

"Lord Dashwood's men came asking for more money," the miller told her. "When I said I had nothing left, they said they'd take Gee-Gee from me." The miller gave a big groan.

"Does he mean his horse?" asked Tom in horror.

"No, his daughter," said Big Jim. "They just have odd names in Max the Miller's family."

Tom was amazed.

"I tried to stop them," said Max.

"I'm sure you did your best," Robyn told him.

"There were just too many of them," said the miller.

"You must rest," said Robyn.

"But what about Gee-Gee?" said the miller. He tried to sit up, but it was too painful, so he lay down again.

"Don't worry," said Robyn. "We'll get Gee-Gee back, safe and sound."

Max the Miller looked up at Big Jim, who nodded. "Robyn-in-the-Hat has given her word, Max," he said. "So it will be done."

Just then, another Green Man arrived. He was dressed as a monk and had a large leather bag.

"What kept you, Doc?" Robyn demanded. "Max is hurt. His cuts need to be looked at."

"And I need to see what I am doing," said Doc. "Bring me a light."

Robyn took Tom by the arm. "Now do you believe us?" she asked.

"Well, yes," said Tom. But he still found it hard to think of his uncle as a bad person.

All his life, Tom had heard such grand stories about his uncle. Now that the time had come for Tom to train to be a knight, he found out that his uncle was an evil man!

"This must come as a big shock to you," said Robyn.

"Yes," said Tom. "But how will you rescue Gee-Gee?"

"Are you going to help us?"

"Me?" said Tom. "How can I help?"

"The men at the castle expect to see you and Able Morris," Robyn told him. "If one or two of my Green Men can pretend to be Able Morris, and if you don't give us away . . ."

"Then I can try to free Gee-Gee as soon as I'm inside!" cried Tom.

"Not just Gee-Gee," said Robyn.

"You could let us in, and we could attack Dashwood Castle and set everyone free!" Robyn exclaimed. "It would save a lot of time if you could open the gate for us."

Tom felt sick. "I'd like to help," he said, "but it seems wrong to open the gate and betray my uncle."

What did his mom tell him? Be brave and true.

"I know how you feel," said Robyn, "but you saw what they did to Max. He's just one of hundreds who have been harmed by your uncle's men."

"Can I give you my answer in the morning?" asked Tom. He was tired.

"Do you give me your word that you won't try to escape?"

"I do," said Tom.

"Then you may tell me in the morning if you will help us free Gee-Gee and the others," said Robyn.

After supper, the outlaws sang songs around the campfire in hushed voices.

Tom soon went to sleep. He woke up when someone put a hand over his mouth.

In the darkness, Tom could barely see that it was Able Morris.

"We must run away," he told Tom. "Come with me!"

Tom gave a groan. He had given Robyn his word. What was he to do?

Chapter 4

To the Castle!

Tom looked at Able Morris. "I can't," he told him.

"Can't what?" asked Able Morris.

"Run away."

"Why?" asked Able Morris. He looked upset. "Are you in pain? Have the outlaws hurt you?"

Tom shook his head. "No, I've given Robyn-in-the-Hat my word that I won't try to escape."

"And I've given your uncle my word that I will bring you safely to Dashwood Castle," said Able Morris.

"Oh dear," said Tom. "Then we both have a problem."

Able nodded at Tom and crept off to the edge of the camp. Tom knew he must follow. The sleeping outlaws could not hear them now.

"Let me think," said Able in a hushed voice.

Who should Tom trust? Robyn-in-the-Hat or Able Morris?

Was Able hiding the truth? Was his uncle really an evil man?

"I know how you can get away from here without breaking your promise," whispered Able Morris.

"How?" asked Tom.

"I shall take you prisoner!" grinned Able.

Then, for the second time in 24 hours, Tom found himself in a sack! This time there was a gag in his mouth, so he couldn't cry out.

Able Morris must have stolen back his own horse. It was the first thing Tom saw as he was let out of the sack. He was dropped on the ground with the blue sky above him.

"I'm not sure if I should thank you or shout at you!" said Tom to Able.

"This way, you kept your word to Robyn," said Able Morris. "You didn't run away. I took you away from the camp against your will."

"But they don't know that," Tom said as he stood up. He sounded unhappy. "Where are we?"

"Look behind you," said Able.

Tom turned around, and there was Dashwood Castle. It was even bigger than in his dreams. It had high walls of thick stone, with a round tower at each corner, and there were armed soldiers keeping watch.

Tom gazed at it. This was Dashwood Castle, and he was a Dashwood!

He felt very proud. But what had Robyn-in-the-Hat told him? And then there was poor Max the Miller. He would ask his uncle about all this as soon as possible.

Tom was very excited. "Can we go inside?" he asked.

"That's why we're here," grinned Able Morris. He got up onto Ferdy and pulled Tom up after him. They rode over a bridge that led to a small outer tower, where they were met by a guard.

"Halt! Who goes there?" asked the guard.

"Able Morris and Master Tom Dashwood," said Able. His face broke into a grin.

"You may enter," said the guard, but he did not smile. He gave a signal to the guards at the main gate of the castle. There was a grating noise, and the drawbridge came down.

They rode across it and through the gateway into the courtyard. Able Morris and Tom had arrived at last.

Just as Tom slid off Ferdy, a tall, thin man in a dark-blue cloak came into the courtyard.

"Why did you take so long getting here?" he wanted to know.

"We were kidnapped by outlaws, Marshal," said Able Morris. He sounded nervous. "But we escaped."

The marshal stared at Able Morris. "So that's your story," he said. "Bring the boy to his uncle. Lord Dashwood wants to see him, and we must keep his lordship happy."

"Y- yes, Sire," nodded Able Morris.

Ferdy was led off to the stables. The drawbridge was raised again.

"Are you Marshal Guppy?" Tom asked the man in the dark-blue cloak. Tom expected him to be bigger and meaner, from what the outlaws had said.

"I am," said Marshal Guppy. "Have you heard of me?"

"Yes, Sire," said Tom. All at once he felt very small and lost in this huge castle with all these people around.

"You've heard good things, I hope," said Marshal Guppy. He gave a nasty laugh. "I'm glad you are well after the bad time the outlaws gave you. Now, go to your uncle!"

Lord Dashwood was much different than Marshal Guppy. He was a big, round man and had a grin on his face.

He was sitting in a huge chair. His left leg rested on a wooden stool. It was bound up in bandages.

"Let me take a look at you, Tom!" he said. "You've grown into a fine lad!" He waved for Tom to come over and gave him a slap on the back and a hug. "Welcome to Dashwood Castle!"

"Hello, Uncle," said Tom. "We were taken prisoner by the Green Men of Gressingham! They said that —"

At that moment, Marshal Guppy strode into the room.

"Time to take your medicine," he said to Lord Dashwood and bowed.

He handed Tom's uncle a goblet, and Lord Dashwood took a long drink.

"Thank you, Guppy," he grinned. "What would I do without you? You're my nanny, my advisor, my marsh . . . marsh-sh-sh . . ." His eyes closed and he fell fast asleep.

"You must let his lordship sleep now," said the marshal. "He's a sick man. Able Morris, show the lad to his room." Marshal Guppy picked up the empty goblet and left the room.

"My uncle's sick? Why didn't you tell me this, Able?" Tom asked.

"Orders," said Able Morris. "Lord Dashwood's in charge of the lives of all the people for miles around. He doesn't want them to think he's weak and can't look after them or give them orders."

"What's wrong with him?" Tom wanted to know.

"He hurt his foot when he was out hunting. Since then, he has never been strong. He spends his time here in his room. Sometimes he sleeps all day."

"It's the medicine that does it," added Able Morris. "I spend my time here with him. That's why he needs Marshal Guppy to take charge of things for him."

"And does Marshal Guppy do what my uncle wants?" Tom asked.

"What do you mean?" asked Able.

He took a large blanket and tucked it around Lord Dashwood.

"Well, it sounds as if Guppy can do what he likes," said Tom. "Marshal Guppy tells people it's my uncle's orders. If the people don't like it, they blame my uncle!"

"That's not true!" said Able Morris. "I'd know if there were odd things going on."

"Would you know?" Tom asked. "You spend all your time in here with my uncle. You don't know what goes on in the villages or in the dungeons."

"Then why did Marshal Guppy take the risk of sending me off to bring you here?" Able asked. "On the way I might have seen or heard something that he didn't want me to know. Why didn't he send one of the guards?"

"Was it Marshal Guppy or my uncle who asked you to bring me here?" asked Tom.

"Your uncle —"

"And Marshal Guppy wants my uncle to think that everything he wants done, is done. So you had to go and fetch me," Tom went on.

Able Morris sat in a chair by Lord Dashwood. "I don't know what to think," he said with a sigh.

"If only I could get to the dungeons to find out if Max the Miller's daughter, Gee-Gee, is there," said Tom.

There was a small sound, and Tom saw a shadow moving outside the door. "Someone was standing there!" he cried. "And he heard what we said! He'll report us to Marshal Guppy, and then we're done for!"

They ran to the door. "We must act quickly," said Able. "Let's look in the dungeons. If you're right about Guppy, we'll tell your uncle everything when he wakes up. Follow me!"

Chapter 5

Time for Action

Able was a very large man, but he moved so fast that Tom could hardly keep up with him. They sped through a maze of passages and down some stone stairs.

Tom knew that he'd never be able to find his way back on his own.

"What happens if they won't let us in?" Tom panted.

"Then you must find a way to peek inside when the guard isn't looking," said Able. "I'll talk to him."

At last, they got to the dungeon.

"Lord Dashwood has asked me to have a look around this place," Able told a sleepy-looking guard.

"Let me see your orders."

"I don't have any written orders," said Able. "I'm Able Morris, Lord Dashwood's loyal assistant. I am not a common soldier who needs written orders."

"Well," said the guard, "I am a common soldier, and I need written orders. I'm not going to risk anything by letting you in . . ."

While the two men were talking, Tom slipped behind the guard's back. He went on down the passage.

There was a thick door at the end. There was a low window with bars on one side of the door.

Through the bars, Tom could see a gloomy room below.

There was straw on the floor. The room was full of prisoners. Hundreds of them. Some had chains. Some were free to move about. Men, women, and children. Young and old.

They all looked thin and dirty.

Tom pressed his face up against the bars. "Psssssssssst! Pssssssssssssst!"

"Who is it?" a prisoner asked.

"Ssssh!" said Tom softly. "Is Gee-Gee, the miller's daughter, there?"

After a while, a small, dark-haired girl was lifted up to the bars. She was crying. She peered through the bars and saw Tom.

"What is it?" she asked. "Is my dad all right? Who are you?"

"I'm a friend," Tom told her. "Your dad is fine. He was hurt, but one of the Green Men is looking after him. The Green Men are going to rescue you all. Be brave. Tell the others that Robyn-in-the-Hat is on her way!"

Gee-Gee was so excited she gave a yell. The guard came running down the passage. There was nowhere for Tom to hide.

Tom didn't try to dodge him. He dashed right at him and then, at the last moment, dove between his legs. The guard fell onto the stone floor with a nasty crunch, and Tom and Able ran away down the endless passages.

At last, Able led Tom into a room
with a large oak wardrobe along
one wall.

They seemed to be alone. "Well?"
Able asked.

"Gee-Gee and hundreds of other
prisoners were there," said Tom. "What
Robyn-in-the-Hat said was true. I know
it's hard for you to believe, but you and
my uncle have been tricked. Dashwood
Castle is evil now. It's the outlaws who
are on the side of good!"

"If that's true, Master Tom, then
the guard outside your uncle's room,
the one who heard us making plans,
will have told Marshal Guppy," Able
explained. "The dungeon guard will
also report us."

"Soon, it'll be too late to do anything," Able added. "Marshal Guppy will lock us up, too. He'll tell your uncle some story to explain why we're not there. Your uncle trusts him."

At that moment, Marshal Guppy stepped out of the wardrobe.

"It will be easy to trick your old fool of an uncle," said the marshal. "He sleeps most of the time, drugged by the medicine I give him. And right now I'm planning a little bad luck for Tom. There will be a lot of blood and broken bones."

"Take the prisoners away!" Marshal Guppy commanded.

Two soldiers grabbed Able and Tom and dragged them off.

Chapter 6

Uninvited Guests

Now everyone knows the most important thing that people need in a castle. Water. Without it, they die!

Dashwood Castle had a large well in a room on the ground floor. The water was as muddy as the water at Tom's house. That Sunday morning, something odd was going on in the well room. Every few minutes, a man climbed out of the well.

Each man carried a sword and a sack. Out of the sack, he pulled a monk's robe, which he put on. He then tucked his sword inside the robe and pulled the hood over his head.

Soon, the room was full of hooded monks. When they were all there, the monks went out into the courtyard.

Tom did not know about the monks until someone looked through the window of his prison cell.

It was Friendly, one of the Green Men of Gressingham, dressed as a monk. His hair was still wet from the well. "Don't be scared, Tom. Help is on the way!" he said softly.

"But you think I'm the enemy!" cried Tom.

"No!" smiled Friendly. "You told the other prisoners that help was coming. You're a prisoner in your uncle's own castle. You're a friend, Master Tom."

He threw one end of a thick rope down to Tom.

Tom climbed up the rope and barely squeezed through the bars of his prison cell. "What about the others?" he asked.

"Big Jim has freed the prisoners from the main dungeon. Your friend Able was there," said Friendly. "The marshal's men only outnumber us by 500 to 1!"

"We must get to my uncle and tell him what's been going on. We must get him on our side," said Tom.

"If only I knew my way around the castle. I don't know how to find my uncle's room."

"Don't worry!" said Friendly. "I have a map." He looked at it. "Now, let me see."

Chapter 7

Attack!

Tom's uncle was amazed when Tom and Friendly woke him up. "Good morning, Tom. What's going on?"

"You've been tricked, Uncle!" Tom told him. "Ever since you hurt your foot and couldn't get around, Marshal Guppy has been doing evil things in your name. He's been overtaxing the peasants and keeping all of the money for himself."

"He's also been putting good, honest people in prison — men, women, and children, too," Tom added. "I saw them there last night."

Lord Dashwood looked at Friendly in horror. "Is this true?" he asked.

"It is, my lord," said Friendly. "I thought you were to blame until Tom told me what was going on."

"I must do something to put things right!" said Lord Dashwood. "Where is Able? Is he one of Marshal Guppy's men, or is he still loyal to me?"

"He's very loyal to you," said Tom.

"I'm happy to hear that," Lord Dashwood said.

"But Able Morris was taken prisoner," Tom went on.

He told his uncle the whole story.

"So the Green Men are here and are setting the prisoners free," said Lord Dashwood. "This is the perfect time to strike back at Guppy. I need your help, Tom. No more talk. Now — to action!"

Soon, the guards and servants were amazed to see his lordship walking around with the help of Tom and Friendly. They were pleased, too.

In the courtyard, something very odd was going on. Some monks and freed prisoners were fighting with the castle guards.

The monks had thrown back their hoods, and it was easy to see that they were the Green Men of Gressingham. They were all enjoying a good fight.

Big Jim picked up two guards and banged their heads together with a loud THUNK!

The outlaws were winning. Then Marshal Guppy rode into the courtyard with a group of armed knights.

"Kill them all!" cried Marshal Guppy as he drew his sword. The knights drew their swords, too.

"Wait!" boomed a loud voice. The knights stood still. They knew that voice well. It was their lord and master, Lord Dashwood.

He limped forward and stood on the stone steps of the chapel. "Stop fighting!" he shouted. Even the outlaws and freed prisoners stopped and stared.

"There will be no killing here today!" Lord Dashwood told them. "But someone may soon hang for the evil deeds done in my name."

"The old fool's gone mad," cried Marshal Guppy. "Why do you think I've been put in charge?"

"I am your lord and master, not Marshal Guppy!" Lord Dashwood reminded everyone.

Tom stood proudly at his side.

Guppy had made a bad mistake.

It was now clear that he had not taken his orders from Lord Dashwood. He had been acting on his own. The marshal knew he was now out of luck. He galloped off toward the gatehouse. "Lower the drawbridge!" he yelled.

The guards did not know what was going on in the castle. They lowered the drawbridge.

"He's going to get away!" cried Tom.

"Don't be so sure of that, Master Tom!" yelled Big Jim.

Everyone rushed to the drawbridge and saw Marshal Guppy stop in the middle. Someone was standing there, blocking his way.

It was Robyn-in-the-Hat herself!

"Robyn! Robyn!" cheered the Green Men.

She nodded to the crowd and then, with a clever twist of her staff, she knocked Marshal Guppy from his horse. He flew off and fell into the moat. He sank like a sack of stones.

"Where did he go?" asked Tom, running onto the drawbridge and looking into the moat. "Is he trying to escape underwater?"

Robyn-in-the-Hat jumped into the moat. She was gone for some time.

When she came up, she was holding Marshal Guppy. They were pulled to safety.

"I can hardly lift him!" Robyn-in-the Hat panted.

When she took off his cloak, she soon found out why. Gold coins fell out of the wet cloak onto the drawbridge.

"He has gold hidden in there!" Robyn laughed.

It was the gold he had hidden away in case he ever needed to flee the castle!

Lord Dashwood walked onto the drawbridge. Able Morris ran out from among the crowd to stand at his side.

"Hello, my loyal friend," said his lordship to Able, with a warm smile. "Glad to see you're safe and sound."

Then he turned to Robyn-in-the-Hat. "Thank you," he said.

"I don't deserve your thanks. I'd like to say how sorry we are," said Robyn.

"If it weren't for Tom, we'd still think that you gave the orders for those evil deeds," she added. "We should have known that you were a good man."

* * *

The next night there was a feast in the castle. All of Lord Dashwood's friends came from miles around. Even Tom's parents were there.

His mother was crying (for joy this time).

People who had heard that Lord Dashwood was sick were happy to find him so strong and healthy. Doc had looked at his bad leg, and it was better.

The Green Men came to the castle, but where was their leader, Robyn?

"Who are you looking for?" asked a voice.

Tom turned and saw a beautiful, young woman in a long, green dress. She sat down next to him at the table. "I'm looking for Robyn-in-the-Hat," Tom told her.

"So you've met the leader of the outlaws?" she asked. "She sounds very exciting."

"She is," said Tom. "Her Green Men kidnapped me, but we became friends."

"Is she beautiful?" asked the lady, with an odd smile on her lips.

"She wears a mask, so I've never seen her face," Tom admitted.

He looked at the lady beside him. She had shining blue eyes.

Tom's uncle banged a golden goblet on the table. "Let's drink to the Green Men of Gressingham!" he cried.

Everyone in the great hall of Dashwood Castle stood up. "To the Green Men of Gressingham," they cheered.

They all lifted their goblets to their lips.

The lady with the shining blue eyes winked at Tom.

Could she be? No, of course not — but then again, she might be.

About the Author

Philip Ardagh is a full-time writer of fiction and nonfiction. He has written more than 70 books, including the Eddie Dickens Trilogy and The Further Adventures of Eddie Dickens.

Philip participates in literary festivals all over Great Britain, and he enjoys watching the wildlife in his backyard. He lives with his wife and one cat, Beanie, somewhere by the sea in England.

Glossary

cloak (KLOHK)—a loose coat

drawbridge (DRAW-brij)—a bridge that raises and lowers to permit or prevent people from crossing

mock (MOK)—false or not real

page (PAYJ)—a boy who is in training to become a knight

ransom (RAN-suhm)—a demand of money to release a person who is held captive

signal (SIG-nuhl)—a sound or action that alerts people

spy (SPYE)—a person who secretly watches the actions of someone else in order to gain information

tax (TAKS)—money that people or businesses must pay to help support a government

Discussion Questions

1. Tom told Robyn-in-the-Hat that he would tell her in the morning whether he would help release the prisoners inside Dashwood Castle. If Able Morris hadn't made Tom escape, do you think he would have helped the Green Men of Gressingham? Why or why not?

2. Robyn-in-the-Hat wore a mask because she led two lives. Why do you think she was only a part-time outlaw? What do you think her "other" life was like?

3. Why did Marshal Guppy trick Lord Dashwood? What did Marshal Guppy gain by tricking everyone?

Writing Prompts

1. How would the story be different if Tom had found out his uncle really was evil? Write about how Tom would have dealt with his evil uncle. Would he have asked for help from the Green Men of Gressingham?

2. It is important to see both sides of a story before making judgements. Write about a time when you were told something about a person that was not true. How did you act toward that person at first? Did you act differently when you found out the truth?

3. Imagine that you have two lives like Robyn-in-the-Hat. What would your two lives be? Write about them and why you would have to keep your lives hidden from each other. What would happen if people found out that you were living two lives?

Internet Sites

Do you want to know more about subjects related to this book? Or are you interested in learning about other topics? Then check out FactHound, a fun, easy way to find Internet sites.

Our investigative staff has already sniffed out great sites for you!

Here's how to use FactHound:

1. Visit *www.facthound.com*

2. Select your grade level.

3. To learn more about subjects related to this book, type in the book's ISBN number: **159889000X**.

4. Click the **Fetch It** button.

FactHound will fetch the best Internet sites for you!